Book Club Edition

WALT DISNEY PRODUCTIONS

presents

The Almost Missed
Christmas

Random House 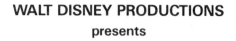 **New York**

First American Edition. Copyright © 1985, 1986 by The Walt Disney Company. All rights
reserved under International and Pan-American Copyright Conventions. Published in the
United States by Random House, Inc., New York, and simultaneously in Canada by Random
House of Canada Limited, Toronto. Originally published in Denmark as JULEMANDENS
VAERKSTED by Gutenberghus Gruppen, Copenhagen, in 1985. ISBN: 0-394-88590-2
Manufactured in the United States of America
90   B C D E F G H I J K

It was the day before Christmas.

Donald Duck and his nephews were going
to spend Christmas in the country
with Grandma, Daisy, and Uncle Scrooge.

Everything was packed and ready to go.
But where were the boys?

"I bet those lazybones are in bed,"
Donald said to himself.

"Hurry up, boys!" he called to them.
"We have to leave soon."

Huey and Dewey were still in bed.
Louie had started to get dressed.
But they were not being lazy.
"My eyes hurt," said Huey.
"My head hurts," said Dewey.

"Me too," said Louie. "But don't let
Uncle Donald know. He won't let us go then."

"We'll be right down!" the boys tried
to shout.

But their throats hurt too.

"Something's wrong,"
Donald said. "The boys
sound strange."

So Donald went upstairs
to see what was the matter.

He heard a loud sneeze
coming from the boys' room.

"Oh, my!" said Donald when he saw
his nephews. "Dewey, you look bad.
Louie, you look worse. And Huey,
you look terrible!

"I had better take your
temperatures," Donald said.

"Just as I thought," Donald said.
"You all have a fever. I must call
Grandma now to say we can't come."
"Oh, please don't!" cried the boys.
"We are fine!"
"No, you are not," said Donald.
"You must stay in bed."

Donald called Grandma.
"The boys are sick,"
he said. "So I'm afraid
we can't come to visit."

Daisy was helping Grandma
in the kitchen.
She heard Grandma talking.
Something was up!

"Oh, dear, that's sad,"
Grandma said to Donald.
"I hope the boys get well
soon. Give them our love."

Grandma told Daisy and Scrooge the news.
"We baked cookies. We wrapped all
the presents. And now they can't come,"
Grandma said sadly. "What will we do?"

"I'll tell you what we will do,"
Scrooge said. "If they can't come here,
we will go there. We'll take Christmas
to Donald and the boys!"

"Grandma sends her love," Donald said
to the boys a little later. "Now, here is
some nice hot milk for you to drink.
Then I will tell you a story."

The milk made the boys feel sleepy.
Donald put on a Santa cap to cheer
the boys up.
Then he started to read the story.

"It was the day before Christmas.
The elves in Santa's workshop were busy.
Would they finish all the toys in time?

"Santa told his reindeer, 'We will make many boys and girls happy tonight.'

"Ho, ho, ho!" laughed Donald.

"Don't I sound just like Santa?" he asked the boys.

The boys were asleep. Donald tiptoed out of the room.

Huey, Dewey, and Louie were dreaming
that they were up at the North Pole.
There was Santa's sleigh and workshop—
and Santa himself with his reindeer!

But in the boys' dream, Santa looked worried.

"Let's ask him what is wrong," Louie said to his brothers. "Maybe we can help."

Santa took the boys to the elf house.

"The elves are all sick," said Santa.
"The toys won't be ready for Christmas!"

"We can help you," the boys said.
"Just show us what we have to do."

"First we'll go
to the workshop,"
Santa said.

Santa showed
the boys what had
to be done.
They fixed
soccer balls,

snorkel sets,

and tennis rackets.

Louie put
tennis balls
in cans.

Huey painted toy trucks.
Dewey got the skis ready.

"You boys are great helpers,"
Santa said. "You have saved Christmas
for all the boys and girls!"

"Thanks, Santa," said Huey, Dewey,
and Louie.

They finished fixing the teddy bears
and the wooden soldiers and the sleds.

Finally all the toys were ready
to be wrapped.

Huey used paper
with trees on it.

Louie picked
red paper with stars.
Snip! Snip! Snip!
went his scissors.

Dewey's paper
had gold and white
stripes on it.

At last all the presents were wrapped.
The boys took them outside.
They helped Santa load the sleigh.

Away went Santa with all the toys.
"Thanks for your help!" Santa called
to the boys. "And Merry Christmas!"

"Merry Christmas!" shouted Huey,
Louie, and Dewey.

Of course, the boys were only dreaming.
Meanwhile, Scrooge, Grandma, and Daisy
were really on their way to Donald's house.
Scrooge's car was filled with food
and presents.

The snow was deep and the air was cold.
But hot tea made everyone feel warm.
"Donald will be surprised," said Scrooge.
"He must be feeling sad," said Daisy.
"I hope the boys are better," said Grandma.

Daisy was right.
Donald was tired and sad.
"Christmas is not going
to be much fun," he thought.

Then Donald heard
a car horn.
"Who can that be?"
he wondered.

Donald looked out the window.
He saw Scrooge, Grandma, and Daisy!
They were busy unloading the car.

"Am I glad to see you!" Donald said.
"Let me help you with your things.

"We must be quiet," Donald added.
"The boys are asleep upstairs."

Grandma and Daisy took
the food to the kitchen.

It was already cooked.
They just had to warm
it up.

Soon Donald's house
looked like Christmas.
The tree was set up
with presents under it.
And Daisy had made
some hot cocoa.

Donald hung up
Christmas stockings.
Scrooge shook
some jingle bells.
"Ho, ho, ho! I
feel like Santa!"
he said happily.

Upstairs, the boys' dream was ending.
Then all at once, the boys were awake.
But they still heard sleigh bells!

The boys' long sleep had made them feel much better.

They jumped out of bed and ran down the stairs.

Had Santa come already?

"Merry Christmas!" cried Daisy.

The rest of the family smiled.

They saw that the boys were better.

The boys saw Grandma Duck, Daisy, and Scrooge—and the beautiful tree with all the presents under it.

Christmas was going to be great after all!

"What a surprise!" the boys cried.

"Open your presents," Daisy said.

Louie's gift was
a tennis racket and
tennis balls wrapped
in striped paper.

Dewey found
a soccer ball.

"Look, skis!"
said Huey.

Where had they seen
these things before?

The boys ran to the window and saw
a big cloud sailing across the sky.
It almost looked like Santa's sleigh.

Of course, their dream
had been just a dream...
or had it?